MAJOR LEAGUE SPORTS

NATIONAL BASKETBALL ASSOCIATION

By Kevin Frederickson

Kaleidoscope
Minneapolis, MN

Your Front Row Seat to the Games

....

This edition first published in 2020 by Kaleidoscope
Publishing, Inc.

No part of this publication may be reproduced in whole or in
part without written permission of the publisher.

For information regarding permission, write to
Kaleidoscope Publishing, Inc.
6012 Blue Circle Drive
Minnetonka, MN 55343

Library of Congress Control Number
2019939026

ISBN
978-1-64519-071-4 (library bound)
978-1-64494-160-7 (paperback)
978-1-64519-172-8 (ebook)

Printed in the United States of America.

TABLE OF
CONTENTS

Steph Curry drives to the hoop against the Los Angeles Lakers on December 25, 2018.

Clash of the Titans

Steph Curry runs down the floor. His feet pass over the Golden State Warriors logo. He is just past the middle of the court. He **dribbles** closer to the hoop. One teammate, Klay Thompson, stands to his right. Another, Kevin Durant, is to his left. Curry stands just beyond the three-point line.

Curry dribbles. A defender is right in front of his face. Curry keeps dribbling forward. Then he goes backward. He picks up the ball. He quickly throws up a shot. Fans hold their breath. It flies through the air. It drops through the hoop!

LeBron James (23) goes up for a shot over Kevin Durant of the Warriors.

The fans rise to their feet. They are cheering for Curry and the Warriors. It is Christmas Day 2018. Golden State is going up against the Los Angeles Lakers.

The Lakers get the ball back. Lonzo Ball dribbles up the floor. He passes off to LeBron James. James drives toward the hoop. No Warrior can slow him down. James gets to the basket. He lifts up the ball with his right arm. He slams the ball through the hoop. The Lakers players on the bench stand and cheer. It is another big dunk from James.

FROM DOWNTOWN

Klay Thompson of the Golden State Warriors gets a pass from Curry. Thompson stops moving. He sets his feet. They are behind a curved line. It's the three-point line. Thompson lifts the ball up. He throws up a shot. Swish! The crowd goes crazy. The Warriors shoot a lot of three-pointers. The shot is very popular in modern basketball.

The Warriors and Lakers are two of the most popular teams in the National Basketball Association (NBA). They have star players. They win a lot. Millions of people watch the NBA's thirty teams each year. Some buy tickets.

FUN FACT
Curry moved into third place all-time for most three pointers during the 2018–19 season.

Others watch on TV or on their phones. The NBA keeps getting more popular. It is partly because of stars like James and Curry.

Klay Thompson, Curry, center, and Durant won two NBA titles in their first two seasons playing together.

CHAPTER 2

Started Inside

George Mikan stands near the basket. His back is to the hoop. He holds the ball for a few seconds. He dribbles. Then, it's time to shoot. He throws the ball in the air. It bounces off the **backboard**. It goes through the net.

Mikan was one of the NBA's first great players. The league began in 1946. The game was different then. There was no three-point line. There was no shot clock. Teams could hold the ball for as long as they wanted. That kept scoring low. Games had fewer points than today.

FUN FACT

Mikan played in the first four NBA All-Star Games from 1951–54.

George Mikan
was one of
the first superstars
of basketball.

Early NBA games were played in small gyms that sat just a few thousand fans.

There were also fewer teams. And games had fewer fans. The fans did not wear jerseys. They wore suits and dresses. There were no black players until 1950. Fans had few ways to follow their team. They could listen on the radio. Or they could read the newspaper.

The game was slower. Teams did not run up and down the floor. No one dunked. Teams passed a lot. Few players took jump shots. They wanted to get as close as possible to the hoop. Then they shot from close range. Coaches got mad at players who took long shots.

THE EARLY DAYS

James Naismith was a gym teacher.
He invented basketball in 1891. He
grabbed a hammer, a nail, and a peach
basket. The peach basket was the
hoop. Then, he got a ball. He divided
his students into two teams. Players
had to toss the ball into the basket.

National Basketball Association Map

1. Atlanta Hawks
2. Boston Celtics
3. Brooklyn Nets
4. Charlotte Hornets
5. Chicago Bulls
6. Cleveland Cavaliers
7. Dallas Mavericks
8. Denver Nuggets
9. Detroit Pistons
10. Golden State Warriors

11. Houston Rockets
12. Indiana Pacers
13. Los Angeles Clippers
14. Los Angeles Lakers
15. Memphis Grizzlies
16. Miami Heat
17. Milwaukee Bucks
18. Minnesota Timberwolves
19. New Orleans Pelicans
20. New York Knicks

21. Oklahoma City Thunder
22. Orlando Magic
23. Philadelphia 76ers
24. Phoenix Suns
25. Portland Trail Blazers
26. Sacramento Kings
27. San Antonio Spurs
28. Toronto Raptors
29. Utah Jazz
30. Washington Wizards

The league started to become more **competitive** in the 1950s. Mikan and the Minneapolis Lakers **dominated**. They won many championship titles. Then they moved west and became the Los Angeles Lakers. That helped the league grow bigger around the country.

The Lakers carry coach John Kundla off the court after winning their third title in four years in 1952.

CHAPTER 3

Bill Russell grabs a rebound away from Wilt Chamberlain (13) in a 1969 game.

Star Power

Bill Russell gets the ball. He is near the basket. Wilt Chamberlain is standing right behind him. Russell plays for the Boston Celtics. Chamberlain plays for the Lakers. He is the biggest **rival** to Russell. It is a matchup of two superstars of the 1960s.

The fans are packed into Boston Garden. Everyone is wiping sweat from their brow. It's hot inside the **arena**. They watch Russell and Chamberlain do battle.

FUN FACT

As of 2019, the Celtics have won 17 NBA titles, the most ever.

In the 1980s, Larry Bird was the Celtics hero. His Lakers rival was Magic Johnson. These teams spent years showing their greatness. They battled for the championship every year. Each team won titles. Fans loved the rivalry of Magic versus Bird.

The 1990s saw one of the greatest sports stars ever. Michael Jordan **starred** for the Chicago Bulls. He led the team to six titles. He clinched the last one by himself. The game was in Utah. The Bulls were playing the Jazz. Utah was up by one. Jordan stole the ball. He got to the three-point line. He dribbled. He lost the defender. Jordan put up a shot. Swish! The Bulls won the series.

MICHAEL JORDAN

Michael Jordan was known as "Air Jordan" because of his dunking ability.

Tim Duncan ended his career with the fifth-most blocks in NBA history.

The San Antonio Spurs were a great team of the 2000s. San Antonio's Tim Duncan got the ball. He turned toward the hoop. He threw up a shot. It bounced off the backboard and in. The Lakers' Kobe Bryant got the ball next. He passed it ahead to Shaquille O'Neal. Shaq slammed the ball hard through the hoop. The Lakers and Spurs took turns in the early 2000s showing which team was best.

It was LeBron James's turn in the 2010s. James had his back to the hoop. He dribbled twice. Then he passed to Dwyane Wade. Wade stood far from the hoop. He threw up a shot. Swish! The fans cheered like crazy. James, Wade, and Chris Bosh teamed up in Miami with the Heat. The team was full of talented stars. They won two titles.

BASKETBALL COURT

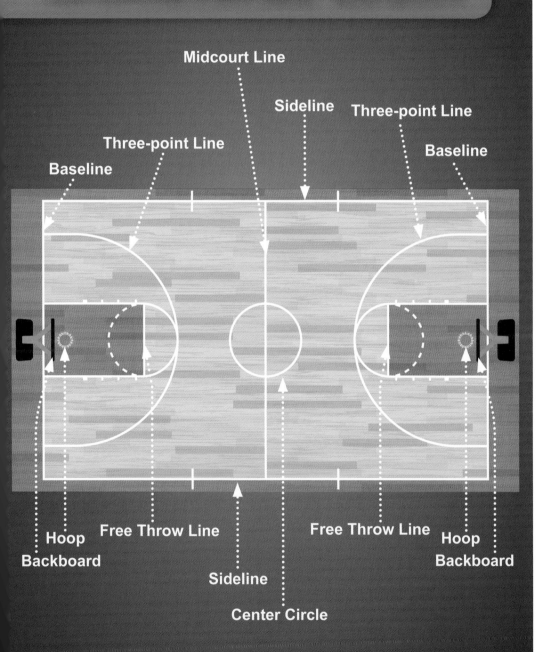

Midcourt Line

Sideline

Three-point Line

Three-point Line

Baseline

Baseline

Hoop
Backboard

Free Throw Line

Free Throw Line

Hoop
Backboard

Sideline

Center Circle

CHAPTER 4

Growing Worldwide

A player dribbles down the floor. He is in high school. He goes quickly toward the hoop. He leaps high. He slams the ball down. He looks just like his favorite NBA players. Fans in the stands erupt. Some stand and cheer. One fan has his phone out to film the amazing dunk.

In North America, basketball has never been more popular. It is especially big with young people. They spend hours on their phones watching **highlights**. Basketball fans follow their favorite players on Instagram. They see what star players are doing off the court.

Fans today have access to NBA highlights and information anytime and anywhere.

FUN FACT

As of the 2018–19 season, the NBA had the most Twitter followers of the four major American sports.

The NBA has changed in many great ways. Once, only men could be coaches. But watching a San Antonio Spurs game shows something different. Becky Hammon is sitting on the bench. She was one of four female assistant coaches in the NBA in 2018–19. And the number of women in key roles in the NBA continues to grow.

It is the middle of the night in China. There are thousands of people staring at a TV. The Houston Rockets are playing. China's Yao Ming starred for the Rockets in the early 2000s. He had to retire in 2011 because of injuries. But fans in China still love Houston because of Yao. He helped make the NBA popular in China.

Due to basketball's popularity in China, the NBA has held several preseason games there since 2004.

MADISON SQUARE GARDEN

HOME OF THE NEW YORK KNICKS

Built: 1968

The Garden is the oldest arena in the NBA as of the 2019–20 season. It was renovated twice, in 1989–91 and 2011–13.

Cost: $123 million

The Garden was first renovated starting in 1989. The $200 million upgrades included adding 89 luxury suites.

Renovation cost: $1 billion (2013)

The Garden's most extensive renovation was completed in 2013. A new scoreboard, new locker rooms, and new seats were just a few of the upgrades.

Basketball seating capacity: 19,812

The Garden's newest renovation set the current basketball seating capacity. It can seat more than 20,000 for other events like boxing.

Luka Doncic, right, is part of the next generation of European superstars, following the example of Dirk Nowitzki, left.

Back in the United States, Luka Doncic of the Dallas Mavericks has the ball. He dribbles near the three-point line. He passes to teammate Dirk Nowitzki. He's just inside the three-point line. Nowitzki puts up a shot. Swish!

Doncic and Nowitzki are both from Europe. So is teammate Kristaps Porzingis. Nowitzki is one of the greatest European-born players ever. Now there are many European players in the NBA.

Fans love the NBA and its players. They live the sport 24/7. The league may have started small. But it is now an international passion.

BEYOND
THE BOOK

After reading the book, it's time to think about what you learned.
Try the following exercises to jumpstart your ideas.

THINK

THAT'S NEWS TO ME. The book talks about the early days of the NBA. How might news sources be able to fill in more detail about what this time was like? What new information could you find in news articles? Where could you go to find these sources?

CREATE

PRIMARY SOURCES. A primary source is an original document, photograph, or interview. Make a list of primary sources you might be able to find about the NBA. What new information might you learn from these sources?

SHARE

SUM IT UP. Write one paragraph summarizing the important points from this book. Make sure it's in your own words. Don't just copy what is in the text. Share the paragraph with a classmate. Does your classmate have any comments about the summary? Do they have additional questions about the NBA?

GROW

REAL-LIFE RESEARCH. What places could you visit to learn more about the NBA? What other things could you learn while you were there?

RESEARCH NINJA

Visit *www.ninjaresearcher.com/0714* to learn how
to take your research skills and book report writing to the next level!

RESEARCH

DIGITAL LITERACY TOOLS

SEARCH LIKE A PRO
Learn about how to use search engines to find useful websites.

FACT OR FAKE?
Discover how you can tell a trusted website from an untrustworthy resource.

TEXT DETECTIVE
Explore how to zero in on the information you need most.

SHOW YOUR WORK
Research responsibly—learn how to cite sources.

WRITE

GET TO THE POINT
Learn how to express your main ideas.

PLAN OF ATTACK
Learn prewriting exercises and create an outline.

DOWNLOADABLE REPORT FORMS

Further Resources

BOOKS

Omoth, Tyler. *A Superfan's Guide to Pro Basketball Teams.* Capstone, 2018.

Rausch, David. *National Basketball Association.* Bellwether, 2015.

Savage, Jeff. *Basketball Super Stats.* Lerner, 2017.

WEBSITES

Factsurfer.com gives you a safe, fun way to find more information.

1. Go to www.factsurfer.com.

2. Enter "National Basketball Association" into the search box and click 🔍.

3. Select your book cover to see a list of related websites.

Glossary

arena: An arena is a kind of stadium, usually smaller and indoors. Boston Garden is one of the most famous arenas in NBA history.

backboard: A backboard is the board that has the hoop connected to it. Tim Duncan's shot bounced off the backboard and went in the net to score two points.

competitive: A league that is competitive has a high standard of play. The NBA became more competitive in the 1950s.

dominate: To dominate means to be the very best in the sport. Michael Jordan and the Chicago Bulls dominated the NBA in the 1990s.

dribble: To dribble means to bounce the basketball off the floor. Steph Curry dribbles the ball toward the hoop.

highlights: Video replays of great moments from a game are called highlights. NBA fans can watch highlights on their phones after the game.

rival: A rival is an opposing team that a team competes fiercely with. The Boston Celtics and Los Angeles Lakers have been rivals for many years.

starred: To star means to be one of the best in your sport. Tim Duncan starred for the San Antonio Spurs for many years.

swish: A swish is when a basketball goes through the basket without touching the rim. Kevin Durant's shot went through the hoop and made a swish sound.

Index

PHOTO CREDITS

The images in this book are reproduced through the courtesy of: Kelvin Kuo/AP Images, front cover (center); EFKS/Shutterstock Images, front cover (background); Rob Ferguson/AP Images, p. 3; Tony Avelar/AP Images, pp. 4, 6; ShengYing Lin/Shutterstock Images, p. 5; Marcio Jose Sanchez/AP Images, pp. 8–9; Benjamin Paquette/Shutterstock Images, p. 10; AP Images, pp. 11, 15, 24–25; Brad Sauter/Shutterstock Images, pp. 12–13; Ververidis Vasilis/Shutterstock Images, p. 13; Red Line Editorial, pp. 14, 26 (chart); Bill Chaplis/AP Images, pp.16–17; AlxMendezR/Shutterstock Images, p. 18; Al Messerschmidt/AP Images, p. 19; Ronald Martinez/ AP Images, p. 20; enterlinedesign/Shutterstock Images, p. 21; wavebreakmedia/Shutterstock Images, pp. 22–23; Matt Sayles/AP Images, p. 24; Pabkov/Shutterstock Images, p. 26 (stadium); LM Otero/AP Images, p. 27; Lightspring/Shutterstock Images, p. 30.

ABOUT THE AUTHOR

Kevin Frederickson is a freelance writer and editor from Ohio. He lives near Cincinnati with his golden doodle, Max.